Edison the Christmas Elf
and the Imperfect Perfect Toy

Edison the Christmas Elf
and the Imperfect Perfect Toy

By Papa V

Illustrations by Melissa Blue

BELLE ISLE BOOKS
www.belleislebooks.com

ISBN: 978-1-9399304-5-3

Library of Congress Control Number: 2014952697

BELLE ISLE BOOKS

www.belleislebooks.com

This book is dedicated . . .

To my wife, Cindy, for her love and support; to Melissa Blue, whose wonderful drawings brought *Edison the Christmas Elf* to life; to fellow author Edward Denecke for his encouragement.

To my daughters, Kimberly, Kristen, and Stephanie, who met the Christmas elf many years ago.

To my grandchildren, Chase, Eleanor, Griffin, Madison, Presley, and Reese, in the hope that they, too, will enjoy the story of the Christmas elf.

And to my favorite animal, the giraffe, who shows up where you least expect to see him.

Chapter One

Once upon a time, not so long ago, in a place as close as your imagination, there lived an elf who dreamed of making the perfect Christmas toy. This is his story…

Knock! Knock!

"Santa!"

Santa Claus rolled over in his bed and looked at his alarm clock. It was midnight!

Knock! Knock!

"Santa!"

Santa pulled the covers over his head.

He didn't want to answer the door. He knew who was pounding on it: Edison, the Christmas elf.

Every year Edison brought Santa ideas to improve Christmas, and although Santa loved new ideas, Edison's ideas were disastrous.

Santa remembered the time Edison had convinced him to let the elves make toys that wrapped themselves. That way the elves would have more time to make more toys. Santa agreed, and everything went just as the elf said it would.

The elves made the toys, the toys wrapped themselves, and that Christmas, the elves did indeed make more toys than ever before.

But there was a problem. Not a small problem, like when a swarm of bees decides to build a hive in your boots.

This was a *big* problem.

When children opened their presents on Christmas Day, their

presents wrapped themselves up again. Children spent all Christmas Day opening their presents, and their presents spent all Christmas Day wrapping themselves up again. The elves never made self-wrapping presents again.

Santa could only imagine what Edison had dreamed up this time. Even though Santa wanted to remain in his comfy bed, he knew he would have to answer the door. He sighed, got out of bed, and put on his robe and slippers. He took a deep breath and said, "Come in."

Edison rushed in and announced that he had made the perfect Christmas toy. The elf invited Santa to visit his workshop the next day to see the toy.

Santa didn't think that tomorrow was going to be a good day. Maybe he shouldn't have answered the door.

Chapter Two

The next morning when Santa arrived at Edison's workshop, he found a tent large enough to hold at least twelve of his sleighs.

Inside, Santa saw a teddy bear so tall that its head touched the top of the tent. The bear's fur was the color of cinnamon. It wore a pair of wire-rimmed glasses, a red bow tie, and a green vest with a gold watch and chain.

The bear leaned on a cane made from the trunk of an oak tree. The head of the cane was shaped like a beehive, and berry bushes and flowers were carved along its sides. It was a magnificent teddy bear.

But there was a problem.

It wasn't a small problem, like when someone glues your shoes to the ceiling with you still in them.

This was an *enormous* problem!

When Santa reached out to feel how soft the bear's fur was, the bear began to topple over—sloooowly at first, then faster and faster and faster!

Santa cried, "Oh no!"

He turned and ran from the bear as fast as he could. But Santa was built for sitting in his soft, green chair and drinking hot chocolate, not for running away from gigantic falling teddy bears. Santa did not run fast enough.

When Edison heard Santa say something that sounded like "Mmph!" from under the fallen bear, he thought it might be a good idea to call the other elves for help.

The elves raced up with coils of rope. They tied the ends to the bear's arms and legs, and along with Santa's reindeer, they pulled on the ropes.

The bear barely moved, and Santa said, "Mmph! Mmph!"

The elves pulled and tugged on the ropes, and the bear began to move.

They pulled and pulled and tugged and tugged on the ropes. They finally freed Santa—seven hours and thirty-nine minutes later!

Santa stood up very slowly. He smoothed out his wrinkled suit, his crinkled beard, and his crushed hat. He took a deep breath and calmly explained to Edison that the bear was wonderful, but it was just too big.

It was too big for a child to hug for comfort when thunder rattled the windows on stormy nights, or when strange noises came from under the bed, or when the closet door creaked open in the middle of the deepest, darkest night.

It was so big that parents would spend all their time rescuing their children from tipped-over teddy bears.

Santa said no more gigantic teddy bears. Edison hung his head. He was sorry his idea had caused so much trouble.

The elves leaned the bear against a nearby mountain, and Edison disappeared inside his workshop.

Chapter Three

Months later, Edison invited Santa to see his latest perfect toy.

Santa came to a sudden stop outside the elf's workshop. He quickly covered his ears as a gigantic, whistling steam engine roared past, pulling thousands of railroad cars along miles of track that curved into the distance behind the workshop. The ground shook as the train thundered across hundreds of bridges and through hundreds of tunnels.

Santa saw railroad cars carrying barrels of root beer and hot chocolate; circus cars with giraffes and elephants; and flatbed cars piled high with licorice logs. It was an amazing sight!

But there was a problem.

It wasn't a small problem, like when a blue bear wearing red tennis shoes and carrying a suitcase knocks on your front door and asks you to show him to his room.

This was a *tremendous* problem!

Shouting to be heard above the roar of the train, Santa told Edison that the train was magnificent, but it was too big, too long, and definitely too noisy.

The parents of any child who got the train would spend years setting it up, if they even found room for it. They wouldn't have any time left over for pancake breakfasts, for making snow angels, or for sledding down scary-fun, steep hills.

But most important of all, if the elves built just one train for one child, they wouldn't have time to make any other toys.

Santa said no more gigantic trains.

Chapter Four

Three years later, as Edison put away the last railroad car, he had an idea for the grandest, most colorful, most perfect Christmas toy of all.

Carrying his ax, a sleeping bag, and a bag of snowflake cookies, he set off for the Great Forest that lay beyond the mountain where the gigantic teddy bear rested.

A few weeks later, hundreds of bellowing bears, raging raccoons, outraged owls, and screaming squirrels showed up at Santa's door. They demanded that Santa return their forest to them.

Santa didn't know what was going on, but he was sure that it was time to visit Edison, even without an invitation.

Behind the elf's workshop, past tilting towers of empty paint cans, piles of discarded paintbrushes, and mounds of sawdust, Santa came to a high wooden wall. It extended to his left and right as far as he could see.

With a boost from several tall brown bears, Santa scrambled up on the wall. The other elves and the forest animals followed him. They discovered that the wall wasn't really a wall. It was the edge of the most colorful and enormous jigsaw puzzle ever made. They couldn't see where the puzzle ended—if it even had an end!

The puzzle was covered with hundreds, maybe thousands, of paintings. Paintings of penguins in bathtubs racing down snow-covered mountains; of beavers building dams of glass behind which sea animals floated in an emerald green sea; and of humpback whales leaping high into the air, trailing rainbow-colored sprays of water. It was a beautiful puzzle!

But there was a problem.

It wasn't a small problem, like when you tell your mom that a giant in pink ballet slippers ate the cake she baked for your father's birthday, and she wonders why you have icing on your face.

This was a *monstrous* problem!

The puzzle stretched for miles, and Santa didn't believe that Edison was finished. Santa hurried off to stop him.

Several days later, Santa found Edison busily working on a painting of a mammoth gold-and-black monarch butterfly.

Santa asked Edison to stop working on the puzzle. He told Edison that the puzzle was already too big to take down any chimney ever built and too big to put under any Christmas tree that ever grew.

Santa told Edison that the animals no longer had a place to live because he had chopped down so many trees to make his puzzle pieces.

Edison stopped painting. He hadn't thought of that. He'd only been thinking of making the best puzzle ever.

Santa thought for a moment, smiled, and said, "Perhaps the animals could move in with you. Yes, that's perfect! They'll live with you until you restore the Great Forest!"

While Edison replanted the Great Forest, the animals made themselves comfortable in his workshop. They ate his snowflake cookies, drank his hot chocolate, ordered pizza, had pillow fights, watched cartoons, and stayed up as late as they wanted.

By the time Edison had packed away the last puzzle piece, the Great Forest had grown back, bigger and better than ever. Then the hundreds of beaming bears, relaxed raccoons, overjoyed owls, and smiling squirrels eagerly moved back in.

Chapter Five

While Edison cleaned up the cookie crumbs, pizza crusts, and pillow stuffing that covered his workshop, he thought about what Santa had said about his toys. They were beautiful, amazing, and wonderful, but they were also just too big!

For years Edison had tried to make the perfect Christmas toy. But all he had to show for his efforts were a teddy bear that fell on anyone who came near it, a train that was long enough to wrap around the Earth twice, and a jigsaw puzzle with pieces so large you needed a crane to move them.

Edison thought and thought about what to do next. When he thought he had finished thinking, he decided to think some more. And just when he thought his head might explode from all his thinking, he had a brilliant idea. He ran out of his workshop to tell Santa.

Knock! Knock!

"Santa!"

Santa Claus rolled over in his bed and looked at his alarm clock. It was midnight!

Knock! Knock!

"Santa!"

Santa pulled the covers over his head.

Santa wasn't sure if he wanted to answer the door, but after a few moments, he sighed, took a deep breath, and said, "Come in."

The elf raced into the room. He excitedly explained to Santa that he had decided that he would stop trying to make the perfect Christmas toy. Instead, he would make huggable bears that fit child-sized laps, trains large enough to roar around a Christmas tree but small enough to fit under one, and puzzles that could be put together in less than a week, or maybe even in a day!

Santa thought this was Edison's best idea of all. He smiled, hugged the elf, and set his alarm clock for Christmas Eve. Edison ran back to his workshop, where he had toys to make, even if it was midnight.

And Santa, his reindeer, Edison, and the other elves—well, they all lived happily ever after making toys that were maybe not perfect, but were just right.

The End?

Maybe not . . .

. . . Edison did have one tiny idea for improving Santa's sleigh. It wouldn't cause Santa any problems, big or little.

The elf only needed to gather a few things before he got to work: 323 feet of wood, 428 feet of blue duct tape, 23 feet of brown rope, 6 bottles of stick-forever glue, a large red button, 427 silver paper clips, 78 waffles, 4 barrels of walnuts, and 1,223 brown flying squirrels.

Edison smiled as he imagined how delighted Santa would be with his improved sleigh.

About the Author

Steven Vaitonis, who writes as Papa V, was born in Chicago, Illinois, and received a degree in biology from the University of Illinois. He lives in northern Illinois with his wife, Cindy. They have traveled throughout the United States and have been to England, Spain, Gambia, Tanzania, and Zanzibar. They have three grown daughters and six grandchildren. Now retired, Mr. Vaitonis has worked for several non-profit organizations, and has spent more than thirty-five years working in research libraries for major healthcare companies. *Edison the Christmas Elf and the Imperfect Perfect Toy* is his first book.

About the Illustrator

Melissa Blue has a degree in biology, and has spent years volunteering in prairie restoration. She works in acrylics, and much of her artwork focuses on the rich diversity of nature in Northern Illinois. *Edison the Christmas Elf and the Imperfect Perfect Toy* is her first children's book. You can find her art at http://www.zhibit.org/profile/melissabluefineart